THE FALL OF XEIROZOGENES
By Jocelyn Almond

When the young and very reluctant hero, Morgbraith, sets out on his quest to slay the dragon Xeirozogenes, it is expected that he will emulate his illustrious, monster-slaying ancestors; but Morgbraith is not so sure, and Xeirozogenes, the great Dragon himself, turns out to be a very different creature from what Morgbraith had anticipated.

The Fall of Xeirozogenes

By Jocelyn Almond

A Short Tale of Endings

First published in Vortex issue 4,
April 1977
First published as a paperback
edition 2009
by Keith Seddon
at Lulu
www.lulu.com

© 2009 Jocelyn Almond

Typeset in Morris Troy and
Morris Golden

All rights reserved. No part of this book may be reprinted or reproduced or utilised in any form or by any electronic, mechanical, or other means, now known or hereafter invented, including photocopying and recording, or in any information storage or retrieval system, without permission in writing from the publisher.

ISBN 978-0-9556844-6-3

To all my friends.

INTRODUCTION

The Fall of Xeirozogenes was first published in April 1977 in the fourth issue of a British science fiction and fantasy magazine, Vortex. At the time, I was twenty years of age, and later that year I married the editor, Keith Seddon.

Over the years, many strange rumours about Vortex have spread abroad, most of them absurdly untrue. One of the rumours was that the editor wrote all the stories himself! This is ridiculous, but it is, however, true that there was a shortage of good work available — only about one in a hundred stories submitted to the magazine was of publishable standard, so that it was necessary to augment this slightly. For this reason I wrote The Fall of Xierozogenes and it was published in the magazine under the pseudonym of Carol Bewley, though the illustrations bore my real name. I chose 'Carol' because I was a great fan of Lewis Carroll, and still am. 'Bewley' was inspired by the stately home, Beaulieu in Hampshire, which I happened to have visited shortly before.

Looking back over thirty years to that young author, I see a vulnerable, shy, extremely naive girl who felt like a frightened misfit in the culture and society around her. Maybe most people feel like that at that age – perhaps it is the nature of youth. In The Fall of Xeirozogenes I expressed my frustrations in veiled form. In the guise of the pompous and preachy Norlan appear the well-meaning but uncomprehending people who advised me practically in a way that I did not wish to go and recommended 'good' jobs, meaning clerical work in offices – a prospect that I dreaded, having already tried being a civil servant for eleven months, before I became an illustrator for Vortex.

Some of the original readers failed to detect the jocular tone of the opening, by which I intended to express my contempt for foolish and hidebound tradition. For those readers, I think, the noble and tragic figure of the dragon Xeirozogenes overshadowed the humour, for in the end, this tale is a sad one.

The transition from childhood to adulthood which takes place in one's late teens and early twenties is seen by many as a time of adventure and excitement, but for me and, I suspect, for many others, it was a frightening, confusing time of rapid change and inconsolable loss. On Easter Day 1977, my dear father died, and my childhood ended. Shortly afterwards, Vortex magazine collapsed, Keith was made redundant as editor, and I was out of work as an illustrator.

The late seventies in Britain was a strange time of social unrest, industrial protest, the Winter of Discontent, and mass unemployment: but most of all, it was the ending of the post-war dream of a land fit for heroes, in which poverty and suffering would be no more, for the welfare state, it had been thought, would care for us from cradle to grave. No one believes that today.

What does a dragon signify? Is it really the terrible monster which, within the story-realm, it is supposed to be? Many things which are terrible within the context of a story actually comprise the very appeal of the story from the reader's point of view. So, murder is horrific in real life, but within the context of a detective murder story, it is the very substance of the story, and provides the basis for entertainment that the reader finds in reading the story. So it is with dragons. Within the story, they are the ultimate evil, but from the point of view of the reader, they are something else entirely: fabulous in both meanings of the word, dragons are exotic, glamorous, thrilling, magical, elusive, and forever unattainable, confined as they are to the fictional universe. In this sense, the wicked dragon can represent our wildest hopes and dreams – especially those which are ridiculous, forbidden, unrealisable. In many ways, The Fall of Xeirozogenes is about the loss of hopes and dreams, but more importantly, it is about the loss of innocence when childhood ends.

Dragons also have another, more significant function: incorrigible villains themselves, they are of course the making of the young heroes who come up against them. My Xeirozogenes recognises that his days of villainy are long gone, but he still takes his role of hero-maker very seriously indeed, and as he bestows his last gift of heroship, it is with that ancient wisdom which is another attribute of dragons. At the end of the story, Morgbraith ceases to be the boy – the term by which Norlan repeatedly and scathingly addressed him – and truly becomes a man, but in a way that neither he nor Norlan had expected, and at a grievous price. Perhaps he becomes a pacifist. In 1977 when the future looked bleak and nuclear annihilation seemed to loom on the horizon, many young people were.

Most stories about dragons are set in the past or in the timeless realm of myth and legend, but the opening sentence of The Fall of Xeirozogenes states clearly that the setting is after the Grand Ignition of 2049. In the context of the story, this event must surely be something disastrous of the dragons' doing! In the context of 1977, however, I think I had in mind the possibility of nuclear war in the real world. The world of Xeirozogenes is, in any case, distinctly post-apocalyptic, its civilisation based on a reconstituted Paganism. On page 28, it is mentioned alarmingly that Morgbraith's father was killed in a Holy War against the Southern

Infidels — a remark which, against the background of today's politics, leaps anachronistically from the page, but which in 1977 could have had no such significance.

More than thirty years later, much has changed, and some things in my life have turned out very much worse than I had feared, even in my worst nightmares; but some of my fears came to nothing, and some of the events of my life have been far better than I could have hoped. Life has made me a far stronger person than that frightened twenty year-old girl could ever have dreamed of being. With Keith at my side, I have somehow struggled through adversity, and like Morgbraith, in the end, I think, we each become our own kind of hero.

Of course, it hardly needs saying, dragons are not really dead, except in stories, which everyone knows are not true! In the real world, dragons are always there, at the heart of imagination, as fresh and wild and thrilling as ever for every storyteller who wishes to write about them.

Once upon a time, not so long

ago, Keith said to me that he wanted to republish The Fall of Xeirozogenes as a small, decorative book, so here it is – for those who remember, and for those who are too young to remember, who are still fighting, and loving, your own dragons!

Jocelyn Almond
Hertfordhire, England
2009

NOTE ON THE DESIGN

The artwork for the cover and the title page (incorporating the design first published in Vortex), and the drawing of the Dragon, are by Jocelyn Almond. The larger decorative borders are by William Morris, from 'William Morris Designs' (Dover 2006); the partial border is from 'Art Nouveau Frames and Borders' (Dover 1983).

The typefaces are also by William Morris: this one is called Golden, and that used for the story is called Troy. They are available in new digital versions from the P22 foundry at http://www.p22.com/

The decorative capitals (by William Morris, again) are included in the Kelmscott Chaucer collection of images, available at
http://www.alfredom.com/

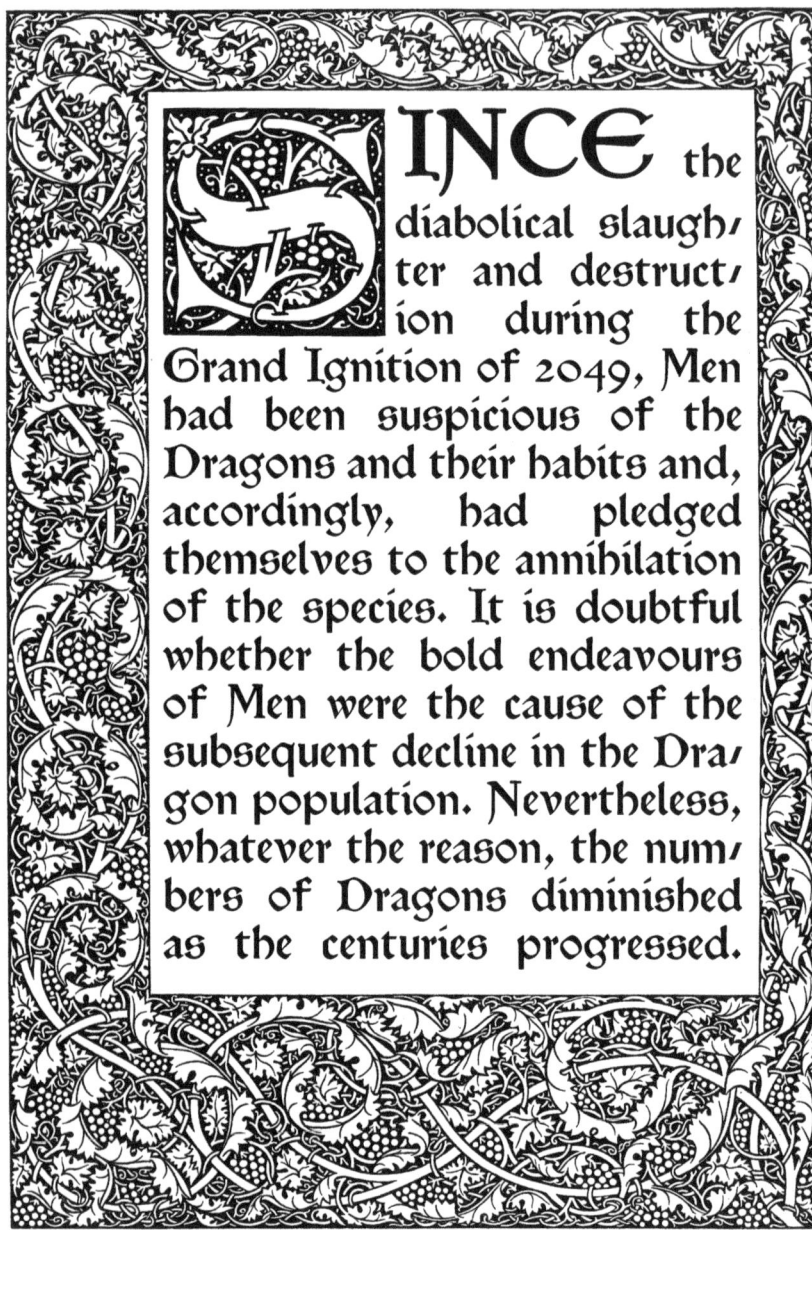

SINCE the diabolical slaughter and destruction during the Grand Ignition of 2049, Men had been suspicious of the Dragons and their habits and, accordingly, had pledged themselves to the annihilation of the species. It is doubtful whether the bold endeavours of Men were the cause of the subsequent decline in the Dragon population. Nevertheless, whatever the reason, the numbers of Dragons diminished as the centuries progressed.

Eventually, only one known Dragon remained alive, that being Xeirozogenes, son and heir of Tzetsedoxyphyll, Despoiler of Twenty Kingdoms.

IT was upon an autumn evening in these latter years that two companions might have been observed, traversing the bleak, ravaged country in the foothills of the Northern Mountains where the Dragons had dwelt long ago, beyond the furthest outposts of Men. One was a warrior in the middle years of his life, broad and tall of stature, who rode upon a white war-horse. His hair and beard were red-gold, indicating that he was born of the barbaric tribes of these Northern lands. He was dressed in the pelts of wild beasts, and many items of rich jewellery that were the trophies of his conquests adorned his person and were woven into his long gold hair, whilst his weathered face bore the scar of an old battle. His belt was stuck with knives, and at his left side was slung a formidable broadsword, the weapon of a fallen king.

IS fellow traveller, who rode upon a fine black gelding, was a delicate youth of pale complexion. His dark garments were trimmed with fur and his cloak was appliquéd in silk with the heraldic designs that disclosed his noble lineage. About his brow gleamed a circlet braided of golden wire, restraining his softly curling dark hair. He was Morgbraith, son of Hengemort the Axeswinger. His companion was his father's old friend and mentor, Elford Norlan.

"YOU KNOW, Boy," said Norlan, "'twas in this same blasted valley that the sire of your grandsires, the Hero Henginsard, slew the Monstrous Thrawn"  "I could not forget it," Morgbraith replied shortly. "Since I was a child I have been constantly reminded of my responsibilities to uphold the family reputation, to be proud that I am descended from Henginsard Thrawnslayer. My father was a Knight of note, and I must perforce follow in his footsteps, whether I would or no" 🍃 The only reply that Norlan would give was to raise his powerful voice in song. The song he sang, provok‑ ingly, was the Lay of Hen‑ ginsard. The mournful notes resounded tauntingly across the grim and lifeless valley through which their horses wended their tedious way. They had travelled since dawn and rested once, and now the setting sun was spilling pools of coppery light over the glassy black, bleak faces of rock that impended on all sides.

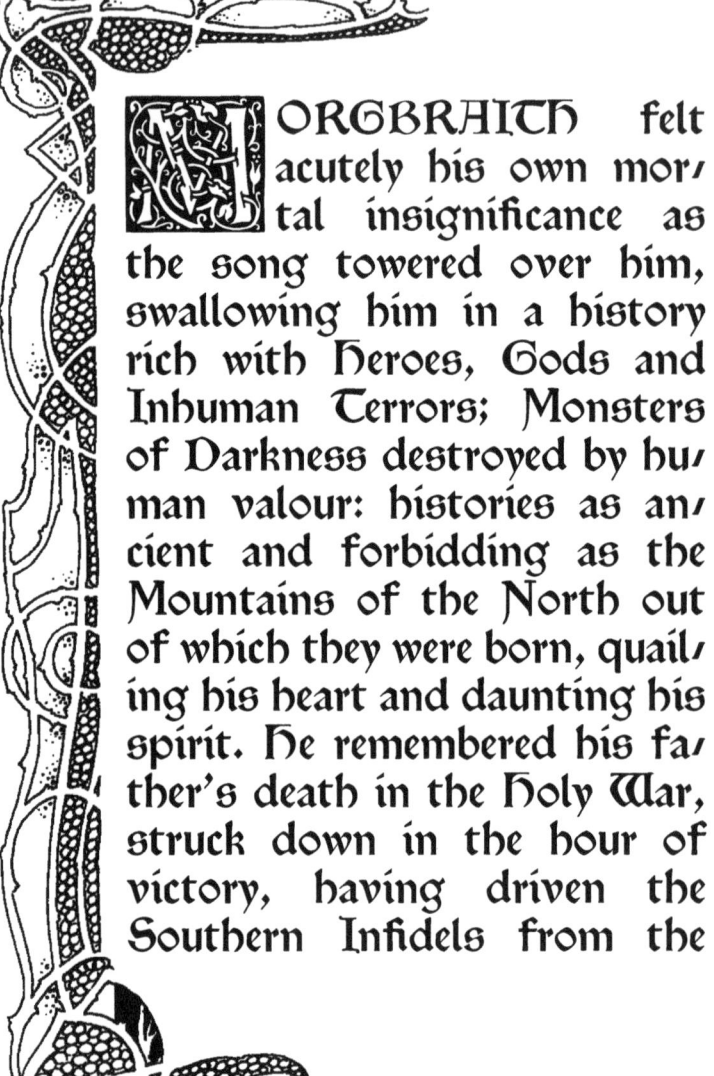

MORGBRAITH felt acutely his own mortal insignificance as the song towered over him, swallowing him in a history rich with Heroes, Gods and Inhuman Terrors; Monsters of Darkness destroyed by human valour: histories as ancient and forbidding as the Mountains of the North out of which they were born, quailing his heart and daunting his spirit. He remembered his father's death in the Holy War, struck down in the hour of victory, having driven the Southern Infidels from the lands of Civilised Men. He remembered the tales he had heard of his grandfather who had killed the Giant of Klerog-gan after only four days of fierce combat, and his uncle who had decapitated the three-headed Beast of Mawkwahn. But it was with unaccustomed tenderness that he recalled his notorious mother, Hilda the Gatecrasher.

TENTATIVELY, his hand sought the sword he carried: Sun-shard, his father's honourable blade, said to be that same weapon that Eastern legends referred to by the mystical name of Palla Sol. For the sake of his father he was resolved to do what must be done to prove his worth as a descendant of his heroic ancestors. For that night, in the Lair of Xeirozogenes, it was his intent to encounter the great Dragon himself, the very last known living Dragon in all the world, and with his father's sword he would slay the monster, or perish in the attempt.

THE SKY deepened to murky purple as the gaunt, black bulk of the mountains obliterated the lingering sunlight, subjecting the still lands to their chill and ancient darkness. Their primeval silence returned as Elford Norlan's song came to an end, and the last sad notes of it withered and died to whispers among the cold stones.

"IS said," Norlan remarked presently, "that the Monstrous Thrawn was the deformed offspring of the Dragons: a degenerate, wingless creature, crawling upon the surface of the earth like a worm" 🖋 "So it is said," Morgbraith agreed 🍃 "And so the Dragons rejected it and disowned it as a child of their noble blood, and cast it out to live alone and wretched in the wilderness" 🍃 "So it is said," Morgbraith assented 🍃 "The Dragons felt no pity for the weak," Norlan observed. "Pity is the sentiment of weaklings for weaklings. Men and Dragons do not pity." He was silent for a while, then, turning to Morgbraith a face ash grey in the ghastly light, he said gravely: "Remember that, Boy."

AND MORG‑BRAITH raised his eyes to the grim, grey crags of the mountains and thought of the ancient, solitary creature that he knew to be lurking somewhere in the darkness of the mountains' shadows: the Dragon which had dwelt there alone, years beyond numbering, the last of his noble race, brooding in the deep caverns of his forefa‑thers. And Morgbraith knew that Norlan knew what he thought, and he said quietly: "I shall remember it."

THEN THEY continued without speaking, and the only sound was the soft breathing of their horses and the dull clatter of shod hooves upon loose stone. Intermittently a wind sighed its chill passage through rocky gullies as they climbed up from the valley and advanced along the mountain path. Above them, a pallid moon shimmered through shreds of blue cloud, and stars brightened icily in the dim, deathless heavens.

HEN the way became too narrow to ride abreast, Norlan took the lead. Eventually the path became too steep and treacherous to ride, and the horses stumbled so that the men were obliged to dismount and continue on foot, wrapping their cloaks about them against the cold of the advancing night, leading their horses by the bridles. Upon their right hand, a wall of rock overhung the path. Upon their left, steep slopes of scree slipped away into shadow.

MORGBRAITH gradually became aware of an emotive fragrance in the wind: a grey scent of old ashes scattered from a cold pyre, yet rich and lingering as the pensive scent of aged books shelved in closed halls. Suddenly, a wild cry that shivered on the brink of his hearing caused his feet to falter, slithering on the broken stones. His horse flinched. He lifted his eyes to the glowering sky and glimpsed the passage of dark wings sliding before the moon, freezing him with the terror of instinct.

"WHAT was that?" he shouted, unable to conceal his fear from Norlan 🍃 The warrior paused, glancing back, waiting for Morgbraith to approach. "You have seen them also?" he asked without surprise. "They are nothing — intangible things that can do no harm" 🍃 "But I saw and heard something — some giant creature. Was it the Dragon?" Morgbraith's anxiety made him persistent 🍃 "No. Nothing but memories. Dead memories." Dispassionately Norlan turned to go on 🍃

"Spirits?" said Morgbraith.

THE warrior answered him without looking back. "There are no spirits here, only the ghosts of the past. They are memories and can do no harm. They are only warnings to caution and prudence in the future."

MORGBRAITH accepted the explanation with the equanimity with which he received all such remarks Norlan made. The barbarian's own life was so firmly rooted in, so much a part of the ancestral myths out of which his dogmatism arose, that it was useless to challenge him with philosophical arguments, especially in the present unfavourable circumstances.

SOMETIMES IT seemed to Morgbraith that other beings inhabited the shadows through which they climbed, and the more he concentrated his thoughts upon them, the more insistently they closed in around him, touching his mind with alien dreams that seemed indeed, as Norlan had said, like memories, though none were recollections of his personal past. Instead, the insubstantial faces of people long dead impressed themselves upon his consciousness. Once he thought he saw the Hero Henginsard himself, his great sword, Arlsbane, at his side, his scarred black armour gleaming wanly in the light of an unseen sun, a blue gem blazing coldly on his brow; but as soon as Morgbraith's gaze fixed on him, his form faded and was gone.

THE stones of the path became larger and smoother as the men progressed with difficulty, the light of the moon often obscured from them by the grotesque eminences of weathered rock that flanked the way.

UNEXPECTEDLY, the path came to an end, and before them spread a vast, smooth shelf of rock littered with white stones, bright in the cadaverous light. Elford Norlan halted, his horse snorting uneasily at his shoulder. "Animals sense the evil we cannot see," he said in a hushed voice. "This is a place of death."

THEN Morgbraith saw that the white stones on which he had been walking were not stones at all, but the bleached and wind-scoured bones of Beasts and Men, carpeting the entrance to the Dragon's Lair.

IN YONDER CAVE," said Norlan, "abides the creature you have come to slay."

SCARCELY had the words left his lips when a deep grumbling arose from the cavern mouth that faced them, echoing dismally among the rocks:

a solemn, awful sound that might have been the stony voice of the mountain itself. "He seems to have detected our presence," the warrior remarked. As he spoke, he took Morgbraith's mount by the bridle. "You must go alone."

HESITANTLY, Morgbraith drew his father's sword. In the cold, pale light, it still glinted golden like the sun, and the soft radiance heartened him. He tried to recall everything he had learned about methods for dispatching Dragons by striking them in suitably soft and vulnerable areas of their anat/ omy. The prospect had never before seemed so ridiculously hopeless, not to mention re/ volting, but one look at the stern visage of Elford Norlan was sufficient to persuade him that he would rather face any kind of death than suffer the scorn of such a man.

"I SHALL wait here," said Nor/ lan. "If you fail to return I shall assume that you are dead, and go back alone."

MORGBRAITH did not reply. His future was too uncertain to consider. Resolutely he made his way across the scattered bones, pausing only once to glance back at the powerful figure of Norlan standing motionless beneath the moon. If he sought encouragement in a parting gesture, he found none. Norlan would never speak a word of farewell, nor wish good luck upon a man for fear of inciting evil influences. Accepting this, Morgbraith turned away and entered the gloom of the cavern.

AT first he thought that the dim bluish light was moonlight shining through the cave opening; but, as he became accustomed to it, he found that his eyes were able to detect the distant interior, which glowed faintly with the same radiance that evidently emanated from the rock itself. The curious aroma he had noticed earlier was stronger here. He coughed. At the slight sound, magnified by its echo, something stirred in the blue shadows, and a deep, soft sound, like a languorous sigh answered it.

MORGBRAITH advanced, but not more than ten paces. The floor of the cave was rent by a wide, sheer-sided chasm, the depths of which were indiscernible in impenetrable liquid darkness. To his right the chasm was spanned by a crude stone bridge, and at the far end of the bridge lay the Dragon.

If the creature had made no sound, Morgbraith would not have recognised his huge reclining bulk. Xeirozogenes' armoured hide was steel blue, gleaming softly like the rocks about him.

SLOWLY Morgbraith approached the bridge, listening intently to the low, steady breathing of the Dragon. He stepped onto the bridge and moved forward warily, expecting at every moment one of the great taloned feet to reach out and swipe him into the next world; but Xeirozogenes appeared to be slumbering. Morgbraith was very close now. He could see the red interior of the Dragon's nostrils, glowing hot and bright with every exhalation, dimming to greyish embers with every indrawn breath. The massive mailed head rested on the folded forelimbs. Between the parted jaws the steely glint of blue fangs was visible.

MORGBRAITH watched the rippling of the lethal crimson spines along the great curved back undulating rhythmically with the creature's slow, even breathing, and as he watched, he lowered his sword until its tip was resting on the rocks at his feet, and within him something faltered, draining his strength and paralysing his will.

AS HE STOOD ON the bridge deliberating, the Dragon's heavy eyelids lifted silently, and from beneath, the old, knowing eyes regarded him with nonchalance. The jaws creaked open a fraction, the nostrils dilated and dimmed as a deep, ponderous breath was drawn. For an instant the rippling spines were motionless. Only the bladed tail stirred, its tip twitching idly like the tail of a reposing cat.

AND Morgbraith looked upon the ancient monster he had come to kill, and he could only look and wonder, his arms falling helplessly to his sides, his weapon forgotten and unheeded, hanging by its wristthong, all concern for himself and the human principles he represented abandoned, dwarfed by the Dragon's greatness.

EIROZOGENES lifted his head. His long tail slithered and coiled over the surface of the rock on which he lay. He began

to raise himself on his forelegs, his scales grating as he moved, his old bones groaning from disuse, and he heaved himself onto the bridge.

AS the terrible head was lowered towards him, Morgbraith saw the soft throat exposed, the golden belly that bore no armour within the reach of his sword, even from where he stood. At that moment he could have slain the Dragon, yet he made no move.

WARM, SCENTED breath rolled over him in a gentle sigh that

scarcely brightened the glimmering nostrils. The golden eyes sunk before him like setting suns in the lowering head, but in their smouldering depths a remote light glittered like the light of distant stars.

So they gazed at one another, the Man and the Dragon, as if they would probe the secrets of each other's soul, and though there was no enmity between them, each knew that the other waited for death.

AT last, Morgbraith moved his arm, grasping his sword, prepared to do what he must do for Honour; whether for that of his noble family, for pride of his heritage or for personal vanity, he no longer knew or cared. Dragons and Men were engaged in an age-long conflict for sovereignty over a world of Beasts, and finally the Dragons had lost. Where Men ruled there could be no Dragons.

HE raised his sword, but as he did so, Xeirozogenes' talons closed over the blade, and once again their eyes met. The Dragon's insouciant expression seemed to have acquired a new quality, but whatever it might be, Morgbraith discerned no trace of bitterness, hatred, or cruelty there. Instead he sensed something akin to sympathy, but it was not pity, for Men and Dragons do not pity.

THEN he thought of Xeirozogenes' years of silent inactivity beneath the mountains: countless years of pondering his own solitary existence with no other company but the memories of what his forefathers had been in their glory. But whatever they had been amounted to nothing now, and all their honour benefited him not at all, and whatever magnificent hoards of wealth they had hidden in their deep caverns were worthless to him who had lain waiting alone there for centuries, waiting for the Man who would come, who, he knew, must come eventually, to put an end to his brooding. But now that death had arrived, it was not a fitting death for the son of Tzetsedoxyphyll.

S MORGBRAITH watched, the Dragon's right eyelid slid slowly over the yellow orb in a significant wink: a profound wink that made a mockery of the pride of Dragons and Men, the futility of Life and Death. Then his talons released the sword and his foot dropped to the ground.

ORGBRAITH waited a minute longer before he turned away and began to walk back across the bridge. Hardly had he reached the other side

when he heard the flapping of enormous leathern wings behind him. He swung round in horror to see the Dragon airborne, the powerful strokes of his golden wings lifting him up to the cavern's lofty roof. Xeirozogenes tossed back his head, opened wide his fanged maw and uttered a cry that was half a laugh of irony, half a screech of agony and wrath. His swirling tail cracked like a whip, and he plunged earthwards, wide eyes blazing, fire coursing from his throat and nostrils. Morgbraith could do nothing to save himself as the

Dragon hurtled towards him. He felt no regret, no anger and no shame. The creature's flaming eyes cauterised all sentiment.

THE REACHING talons were inches from the Man, when suddenly Xeirozogenes furled his sweeping wings and dropped. Beneath him the chasm gaped, inviting him to oblivion. His eyes closed in ultimate resignation; he drew in his great limbs, and fell without a sound into the ageless dark.

FOR A LONG TIME afterwards, Morg-braith stood on the edge of the chasm, staring despondently into the inscrutable gloom, contemplating the mysteries that would remain mysteries now, and the untold stories that had been lost forever with the wisdom and knowledge of Xeirozogenes as he hurled himself to an unseen death. The Age of Monsters and the Heroes of myths had died with him.

CALMLY, Morgbraith lifted his father's sword, Sunshard, noticing for a moment the pale reflection of his own face in its polished, unsullied blade, wondering for a moment if he really knew himself as an individual or merely as a poor reflection of his ancestors and their heroism. Then, with a deliberate gesture, he cast it from him into the chasm and watched its swift descent like a fragment of sunlight through a timeless night, spinning, falling, into the shadows where the last Dragon fell.

NOTE ON THE TYPEFACES

Main text is set in Morris Troy.

Introduction is set in Morris Golden.

Both fonts are available from the P22 Foundry, from whom we learn:

'William Morris (1834-1896) was probably the most influential figure in the Arts & Crafts and private press movements of the late 19th and early 20th centuries. In reaction to the increasing lack of quality that the industrial revolution brought on, Morris sought a return to the ideals of the medieval craftsman. Dissatisfied with the commercially available typefaces of the day, he undertook the design of the fonts for his Kelmscott Press books himself.'

http://www.p22.com/products/morris.html

THE FALL OF XEIROZOGENES
By Jocelyn Almond

When the young and very reluctant hero, Morgbraith, sets out on his quest to slay the dragon Xeirozogenes, it is expected that he will emulate his illustrious, monster-slaying ancestors; but Morgbraith is not so sure, and Xeirozogenes, the great Dragon himself, turns out to be a very different creature from what Morgbraith had anticipated.

Jocelyn Almond is an author and tutor, and lives in Hertfordshire, England. She is married, and has a PhD in philosophy.

FANTASY

www.ingramcontent.com/pod-product-compliance
Ingram Content Group UK Ltd.
Pitfield, Milton Keynes, MK11 3LW, UK
UKHW041434180426
11947UKWH00007B/430